W9-BKM-886

Dear Dragon Goes to the Market

by Margaret Hillert
Illustrated by David Schimmell

NORWOOD HOUSE PRESS

DEAR CAREGIVER,

The *Beginning-to-Read* series is a carefully written collection of classic readers you may remember from your own childhood. Each book features text comprised of common sight words to provide your child ample practice reading the words that appear most frequently in written text. The many additional details in the pictures enhance the story and offer the opportunity for you to help your child expand oral language and develop comprehension.

Begin by reading the story to your child, followed by letting him or her read familiar words and soon your child will be able to read the story independently. At each step of the way, be sure to praise your reader's efforts to build his or her confidence as an independent reader. Discuss the pictures and encourage your child to make connections between the story and his or her own life. At the end of the story, you will find reading activities and a word list that will help your child practice and strengthen beginning reading skills.

Above all, the most important part of the reading experience is to have fun and enjoy it!

Shannon Cannon

Shannon Cannon,
Literacy Consultant

Norwood House Press • P.O. Box 316598 • Chicago, Illinois 60631
For more information about Norwood House Press please visit our website at
www.norwoodhousepress.com or call 866-565-2900.

LIBRARY OF CONGRESS CATALOGING-IN-PUBLICATION DATA

Hillert, Margaret.
  Dear dragon goes to the market / by Margaret Hillert ; illustrated by David Schimmell.
    p. cm. -- (A beginning-to-read book)
  Summary: "A boy and his pet dragon visit the market and see all of the different foods and colors it has to offer"--Provided by publisher.
    ISBN-13: 978-1-59953-347-6 (library edition : alk. paper)
    ISBN-10: 1-59953-347-2 (library edition : alk. paper)
  [1. Dragons--Fiction. 2. Grocery shopping--Fiction.] I. Schimmell, David, ill. II. Title.
PZ7.H558Ded 2010
[E]--dc22

                                    2009031725

Manufactured in the United States of America in North Mankato, Minnesota.
160N—072010

I have to get something
for us to eat.
Do you want to go with me?

Yes, yes, Mother.
I want to go with you.
Where will we go?

4

There is a good spot.
You will see.
Come on. Come on.

Oh, oh—
Look at all this!

You can do this.
It will be a big help.

9

Yes, Mother.
We can help you.
We like to help.
This will be fun.

Oh, this looks good.
Do we want this?

These are green BEANS.
Yes, we want some.
BEANS are good for us.

And look here.
Oh, boy! APPLES!
Can we get some APPLES?

Yes.
We will get some APPLES.

The TOMATOES are red.
They are so good to eat.
We will get TOMATOES, too.

TOMATOES

17

Now what can we get, Mother?

Do you like CARROTS?
We can get CARROTS.

CARROTS

Oh, yes.
I like CARROTS.
Big, orange CARROTS.

There is something yellow.
Yellow CORN.
Can we get some CORN?

I guess so.
It can go in here.

I want something pretty, too.
Look for something pretty.

There, Mother. There.
See the pretty FLOWERS.
You can get FLOWERS.

25

Yes, we will get FLOWERS.
Now we can go.

Here you are with me.
And here I am with you.
What a good day, dear dragon.

The following activities support the findings of the National Reading Panel that determined the most effective components for reading instruction are: Phonemic Awareness, Phonics, Vocabulary, Fluency, and Text Comprehension.

Phonemic Awareness: The /a/ sound

1. Say the word **apple** and ask your child to repeat the beginning sound. Say the word **can** and ask your child to repeat the middle sound. Say it slowly to help your child identify the middle /**a**/ sound.

2. Explain to your child that you are going to say some words and you would like her/him to give you a thumbs-up if s/he hears the short /**a**/ as in apple or can, or a thumbs-down if it is not the short /**a**/ sound.

ate (↓)	at (↑)	cap (↑)	cape (↓)
mat (↑)	mate (↓)	vane (↓)	van (↑)
sad (↑)	sand (↑)	grass (↑)	game (↓)

Phonics: Word Ladder

Word ladders are a fun way to build words by changing just one letter at a time. Write the word **am** on a piece of paper and give your child the following step-by-step instructions (the letters between the / / marks indicate that you are to give the sound as a clue rather than providing the actual letter):

- Add the /**b**/ sound to the beginning of the word. What do you have? (bam)
- Change the /**m**/ to a /**t**/. What do you have? (bat)
- Change the /**b**/ to a /**p**/. What do you have? (pat)
- Change the /**t**/ to an /**n**/. What do you have? (pan)
- Change the /**p**/ to a /**k**/. What do you have? (can)
- Change the /**k**/ to a /**f**/. What do you have? (fan)

Vocabulary: Story-related Words

1. Write the following words on sticky note paper and point to them as you read them to your child:

apples	beans	carrots	corn
flowers	orange	tomatoes	yellow

2. Mix the words up. Say each word in random order and ask your child to point to the correct word as you say it.

3. Mix the words up again and ask your child to read as many as he or she can.

4. Ask your child to place the notes on the correct page for each word, i.e. **apples** goes on the page apples are talked about.

Fluency: Choral Reading

1. Reread the story with your child at least two more times while your child tracks the print by running a finger under the words as they are read. Ask your child to read the words he or she knows with you.

2. Reread the story aloud together. Be careful to read at a rate that your child can keep up with.

3. Repeat choral reading and allow your child to be the lead reader and ask him or her to change from a whisper to a loud voice while you follow along and change your voice.

Text Comprehension: Discussion Time

1. Ask your child to retell the sequence of events in the story.

2. To check comprehension, ask your child the following questions:

  • Why did the mother and boy put the wagon in the car?

  • What did the boy and his mother buy that wasn't food?

  • Where does your family buy food? How is it like the market in the story? How is it different?

WORD LIST

Dear Dragon Goes to the Market uses the 61 pre-primer and 7 new vocabulary words listed below. This list can be used to practice reading the words that appear in the text. You may wish to write the words on index cards and use them to help your child build automatic word recognition. Regular practice with these words will enhance your child's fluency in reading connected text.

a	eat	like	spot	yellow
all		look(s)		yes
am	for		the	you
and	fun	me	there	
are		Mother	these	
at	get		they	**New**
	go	now	this	**Vocabulary**
be	good		to	**Words**
big	green	oh	too	
boy	guess	on		
			us	apples
can	have	pretty		beans
come	help		want	carrots
	here		we	corn
day		red	what	flowers
dear	I	see	where	orange
do	in	so	will	tomatoes
dragon	is	some	with	
	it	something		

ABOUT THE AUTHOR Margaret Hillert has written over 80 books for children who are just learning to read. Her books have been translated into many different languages and over a million children throughout the world have read her books. She first started writing poetry as a child and has continued to write for children and adults throughout her life. A first grade teacher for 34 years, Margaret is now retired from teaching and lives in Michigan where she likes to write, take walks in the morning, and care for her three cats.

Photograph by Glenna Washburn

ABOUT THE ADVISER Shannon Cannon contributed the activities pages that appear in this book. Shannon serves as a literacy consultant and provides staff development to help improve reading instruction. She is a frequent presenter at educational conferences and workshops. Prior to this she worked as an elementary school teacher and as president of a curriculum publishing company.